SHEN RODDIE was born in Singapore. She graduated with a degree in History and began her career as a journalist, interviewing the first men to land on the moon! She lived in Buenos Aires, Argentina and Holland before settling back in Oxford, England. Her previous books include *Hatch Egg, Hatch!*, *Mrs Wolf*, and *Too Close Friends* published by Frances Lincoln.

KADY MACDONALD DENTON was born in Toronto, Canada. She studied Fine Arts at the University of Toronto and now teaches art for children at the Brandon Allied Arts Centre, Manitoba where she lives. She is a highly successful children's illustrator and her previous books include *'Til All the Stars Have Fallen* and *The Kingfisher Children's Bible*. *Toes are to Tickle* is her first book for Frances Lincoln.

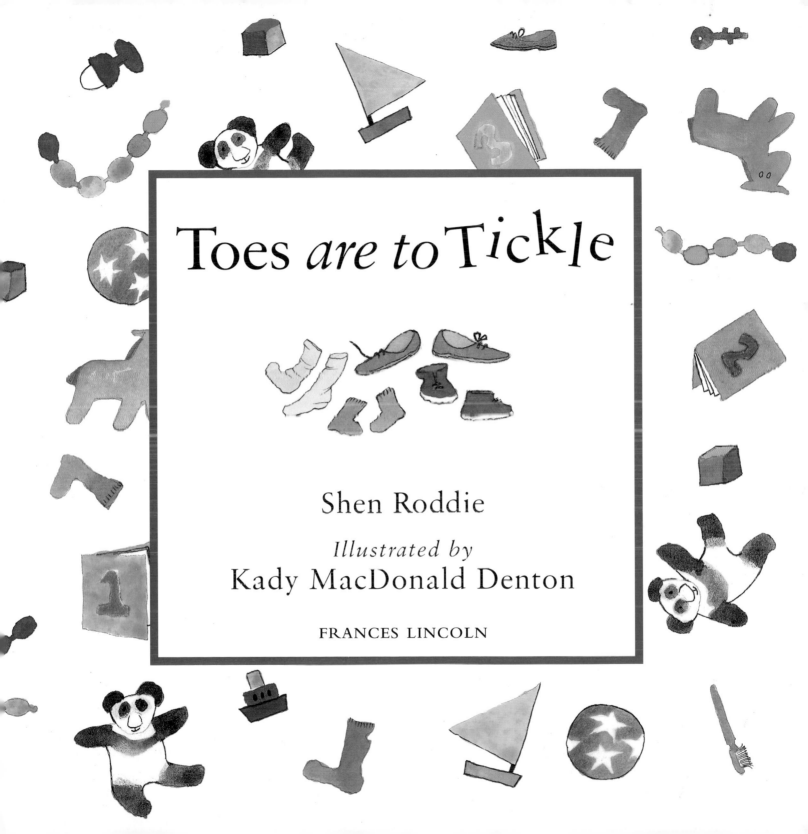

Toes *are to* Tickle

Shen Roddie

Illustrated by
Kady MacDonald Denton

FRANCES LINCOLN

Morning is for waking up!

An egg is to dip.

Bread is for
more jam, please.

Milk is to give
some to the cat.

Clothes are for putting on...

and pulling off.

A mirror is for
making faces.

Toes are to tickle.

Shoes are for taking feet out for a walk.

A pushchair is for pushing.

A see-saw is for feeling
funny in the tummy.

Ducks are to feed.

Birds are
to chase.

Flowers are
to smell.

A tree is
to hide
behind.

Wind is to
blow in
your face.

Laughing is so everyone
knows you're happy.

Blankets are for making tents.

Chairs are for climbing.

Boxes are to see what's in them.

A handbag is to empty.

Books are to choose from.

Toys are for taking out.

A cat is to love.

Peas are for
counting.

Jelly is for
wobbling.

Teeth are to brush up and down.

A bath is for sailing.

Daddy is
for one
last ride.

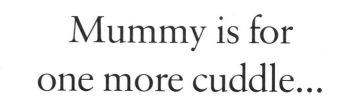

Mummy is for
one more cuddle...

one more story...

and kissing good night.

Good night!

MORE PICTURE BOOKS IN PAPERBACK FROM FRANCES LINCOLN

GOODNIGHT GOZ
Steve Weatherall
Baby Goz leaves his mother's side to go for a walk in the deep, dark night.
There he meets a host of creatures and finds that the nocturn world is full of surprises.
In this fun lift-the-flap book, children can discover along with Goz what happens
on the farm after dark.

ISBN 0-7112-1020-9 £4.50

Suitable for National Curriculum English - Reading, Key Stage 1
Scottish Guidelines English Language - Reading, Talking and Listening, Level A

ANNIE ANGEL
Susie Jenkin-Pearce
When Annie gets angel wings for Christmas she tries hard to be angelic,
but somehow things never turn out quite right. A heart-warming story
which will delight and amuse children everywhere.

ISBN 0-7112-1083-7 £4.99

Suitable for National Curriculum English - Reading, Key Stage 1
Scottish Guidelines English Language - Reading, Level A

OLD MACDONALD
Jessica Souhami
Old MacDonald's farm is full of surprises. What's that in the pram?
Who's flying a plane? What has four arms and goes 'beep'? Lift the five
surprise flaps and see for yourself - then open out the final page
for a deafening finale.

ISBN 07112-1086-1 £4.99

Suitable for National Curriculum English - Reading, Key Stage 1
Scottish Guidelines English Language - Reading, Talking and Listening, Level A

Frances Lincoln titles are available from all good bookshops.
Prices are correct at time of publication, but may be subject to change.